Still the Sirens

*Joyce
Warm good wishes
Sincerely
Dennis Brutus
Nov. 1997,*

Dennis Brutus

Pennywhistle Press
Santa Fe
1993

Poems from this collection have previously appeared in the following publications: *Extra*, (Fairness & Accuracy in Reporting), Human Rights and the Media; Fantome Press; *Words on the Page, The World in Your Hands; The Gar*, "Literature and Liberation", #35; *African Literature Association Bulletin*, Vol. 19, #1; *The Journal of Law and Religion*, Valparaiso University Symposium: "Thoughts on the Shaping of Post-Apartheid South Africa"; *From South Africa* (Northwestern University, TriQuarterly, & University of Chicago Press); *Southern African Review of Books*; Staffrider, Johannesburg and, *Directory of Resources on Southern Africa*.

Printed in the United States of America
by Cloud Bridge Printing, Santa Fe, New Mexico

ISBN: 0-938631-09-8

For additional copies, address orders to: Harbinger House
                                               P.O. Box 42948
                                               Tucson, AZ 85733-2948
                                               Phone: (602) 326-9595
                                               Fax: (602) 326-8684

Note: Poems with the following mark: ~
at the bottom of the page are continued on the next page.

Contents

Introduction

This book has been long in the making, but so has the creativity, life experience, and spiritual energy that informs it. The journey of the world's great poets is, in most cases, a long and arduous one filled with self-revelation. In the case at hand, the revelations are tempered by a committed life of struggle against oppression. So, in a sense, this collection of lays or poems is the blueprint of a spirit dedicated to democracy and freedom. These poems can be turned to again and again as South Africa continues to inhabit the headlines of the world. For it seems reasonable to conclude that South Africa will continue to be that place that challenges the human spirit to transform the furor that resides there, has resided and will continue to reside there for some time.

Indeed, South African society appears as a grandiose passion play that has all the components of the universal issues that beset humanity the world over. Thus, in involving ourselves in the transformation of South African society in either word or deed, hopefully both, we in some sense remake ourselves and our indigenous communities.

To enter his book is to enter not only the mind and heart of Dennis Brutus, but the mind and heart of South Africa as well! In our immediate lives, there will continually be a new crisis in South Africa, and a new crisis in America as a result of America's South African foreign policy, at least as long as Blacks, Browns, Reds and Yellows are effectively denied a role in that foreign policy.

Yet somehow, we, as individuals and ammunition, must remain sane both in our interior world and our external world. Perhaps the best way to achieve that sanity is to be informed enough, open enough, outraged enough to be on the side of justice, righteousness, and truth. One way of reaching that goal is to, above all, LISTEN TO THE POETS! The poet is at his/her best, the mouthpiece of the divine, even when he or she may not legitimately be over occupied with divine!

So we enter into the terror and beauty of that turbulent society with the master craftsman, Dennis Brutus, and we witness and marvel and weep and pray and dream at the wonder of a land struggling for its fate to give the world something only it can give, something only for which it has paid the supreme price.

Thank you Dennis Brutus for surviving to sing for us . . . to sing . . . to sing . . . to sing.

Once, Dennis Brutus and I met at Philadelphia International Airport in preparation to having dinner together. While waiting for the train shuttle into the city, our conversation was filled with a number of topics. The topic of the hour concerned the impending release of Nelson Mandela, symbolic and titular head of the African National Congress, jailed for 27 years in South Africa. Brutus reflected on how he had known Mandela in South Africa prior to both of their imprisonments; later, how when Mandela was a fugitive, he helped hide him out in his home and finally, how once imprisoned, they broke stones together on Robben Island.

As the darkness closed in, consuming the orange blush of evening, Brutus recalled a time when he gave his first political speech, while yet a school teacher in Port Elizabeth, opposing the forced relocation of a Black settlement. That day, according to Brutus, he really roused the gathering assembled to hear his impassioned address. Afterwards, a friend, who had known Brutus for some years and watched his political evolution, remarked that while he had certainly been impressive that day, did he think he had the stamina and endurance to be the long distance runner in the struggle against apartheid.

Obviously, the comment moved and challenged Brutus immensely, in that, decades later, he would find it meaningful to impart the tale to me. The poems found in Dennis Brutus' twelfth book of poetry illuminate his determination to not only endure the rigors of apartheid, i.e., imprisonment, gunshot wound to the back and 'the desolation of exile,' but to overcome it as well.

Near the beginning of this chapbook, in a section dealing with endurance, Brutus says

> "Endurance... is the ultimate virtue—more,
> the essential thread
> on which existence is strung
> when one is stripped to nothing else
> and not to endure is to end in despair."

This attitude then becomes the lynchpin upon which the strength of "Sirens" rests. Here in America, which is so very good at buying off, compromising, betraying, or outright murdering progressive elements, it becomes of utmost importance to survive with integrity to do one's work. So many of our artists and activists become overwhelmed by an insidious despair that leads to over-indulgence in drink, drugs, food or lust, such as to result in destruction.

Such is not the case with Brutus, with the sirens' wail undiminished, he never fails to realize the necessity of continued struggle.

> "Still the sirens stitch the night air with terror...
> still they weave the mesh
> that traps the heart in anguish,
> flash bright bars of power
> that cage memory in mourning and loss."

And in yet another poem included in the endurance section, Brutus seems to be telling us of the kind of stamina required in the throes of exile:

> "... the lashes now, and the labors
> are different but still demand,
> wound and stretch to breaking point:
> and I still snap back, stubbornly."

Brutus is a man who has no time for self-destruction. He no longer smokes cigarettes and is rarely seen drinking anything alcoholic. As he says in another line from the sequence on endurance, "I coil my energies and wait."

"Sirens" is a gathering of moments gleaned from a spirit who has the patience of a stone. The language is sparse, to the point, emotional. There is spring in these poems balanced by the blight of winter. There is the summer of love in these poems and the beauty of autumns. The affairs of humanity are interwoven with the affairs of nature. Neither is separate, they are one. For Brutus, elements of the natural world become symbols and statements casting light on the political aspects of society. In a poem called "Hope", he writes: ". . . one twig shows a green flag of hope" and in another poem:

> "Fall's colors signal
> the cycle's onward movement. . . ."

"Sirens" is a work that is seasonal in its approach to understanding not only the political climate of societies, but also the birth, decline and death of beauty and creators of beauty. Always between absolute destruction and continued civilization, stand those people, places and things that act as measures of salvation, yet keep us from the abyss another year, another month, another week, another day, another hour. Perhaps such an instinct inspired Brutus to write:

> ". . . but there were also these instants
> of unearned, unexpected beauty
> that momentarily redeemed the world."

Such moments are the arc of rainbows, dynamic thunderheads towering over landscapes and "small wildflowers struggle/among spent bullet casings. . . ." —the knowledge that as Brutus says in his poem "Tomorrow":

". . . the barbed wire
and barricades will be gone."

No hatred stares out from this collection, only a profound love for the enigma of humanity, a profound respect for the mystery of Nature of God, a deep conviction that the only certainty is change and perhaps, JUSTICE.

The day after our birthday dinner during a gathering at Community College of Philadelphia for Black Writers, word came that Nelson Mandela would be released. Brutus heard the news (with the same ear, I might add, that once heard the rap of steel on stone of Mandela's hammer on Robben Island). Both activists-revolutionists had lived to witness yet another of life's revelations or redemptions . . . Brutus speaks of it thusly,

". . . you swung your hammer, grimly stoic
facing the dim path of interminable years
now, vision blurred with tears
we see you step out to our salutes
bearing our burden of hopes and fears
and impress your radiance
on the grey morning air."

Even as this introduction is concluded, Apartheid still stomps/romps/pounds/astounds the global village. Passbooks, barking dogs, teargas, truncheons and shackles still mar the furniture of our living rooms. Between this reality and something called a future exists our hearts. What will become of our hearts, what will become of us, can perhaps be guessed at following the map found within the pages of "Still the Sirens."

Lamont B. Steptoe
Poet/Publisher
Whirlwind Press

"Every artist, every scientist must decide where he stands. There are no impartial observers. The artist must elect to fight for freedom or slavery. I have made my choice. I had no alternative."

Paul Robeson

"In a country which denies that men and women are human, where the Constitution excludes them as sub-humans, the creative act is an act of dissent and defiance: creative ability is a quintessential part of being human: to assert one's Creativity is also to assert one's Humanity. This is a premise on which I have acted all my life and it is the premise I have offered to others as an inspiration."

Dennis Brutus

STILL THE SIRENS

Still the sirens
stitch the night air with terror—
pierce hearing's membranes
with shrieks of pain and fear:

still they weave the mesh
that traps the heart in anguish,
flash bright bars of power
that cage memory in mourning and loss.

Still sirens haunt the night air.

Someday there will be peace
someday the sirens will be still
someday we will be free.

ENDURANCE

". . . is the ultimate virtue—more,
the essential thread
on which existence is strung
when one is stripped to nothing else
and not to endure is to end in despair."

I.

Cold floors
bleak walls
another anteroom:
another milestone behind
fresh challenges ahead:
in this hiatus
with numb resolution
I coil my energies
and wait.

II.

Stripped to the waist
in ragged pantaloons
long ago I sweated over bales,
my stringy frame—strained—
grew weary but sprang back
stubbornly
from exhaustion:
the lashes now,
and the labors are different
but still demand,
wound and stretch to breaking point:
and I still snap back, stubbornly.

~

III.

All day a stoic
at dawn I wake, eyelids wet
with tears shed in dreams.

IV.

My father, that distant man,
grey hair streaked with silver,
spoke of St. Francis of Assisi
with a special timbre in his voice:
loved him not, I think, for the birds
circling his head, nor the grace
of that threadbare fusty gown
but for his stigmata: the blood
that gleamed in the fresh wounds
on his palms and insteps:
in my isolation cell in prison,
the bullet wound in my side still raw,
those images afflicted me.

V.

When we shook hands in the Athenian dusk
it closed a ring that had opened twenty-four years before
when a wisp of off-key melody had snaked into my grey cell
whistled by a bored guard in the sunlit afternoon outside:
it circled the grey walls like a jeweled adder
bright and full of menace and grew
to a giant python that encircled me, filling the cell
then shrank and entered me where it lay
coiled like my gut, hissing sibilantly
of possession;
twice I breathed death's hot fetid breath
twice I leaned over the chasm, surrendering
till some tiny fibre at the base of my brain

~

protested in the name of sanity and dragged me
from the precipice of suicide that allured
with its own urgent logic

Our hands meeting, uncordially, your gaze
quizzical, perhaps affronted
sealed a circle in the gathering dusk,
like the ring of dark waves advancing
on the island's jagged shore
and the dark enclosure of wire
whose barbs are buried in my brain.

VI.

Wormwood grey shadows take shape
as night drains from the moon:
objects assume outlines
and some backdrop is suggested
and still the noose of time's expiring closes in

shapes, like bats-upended
hover and circle
holy men chanting their mantras
as darkness dissolves
in a purgatorial stasis.

VII.

In the air pungent with asepsis
the raucous guards swagger
their uniforms and holsters bulk
in a perennial twilight
the sweat of newly dead corpses
makes rigid the smoke-laden fug
the collapsed lung labors stertoriously
strained iterations of emergencies
thread the air like steel bobbins
stitching towards finality, mortality

~

corpselike, in the gloom
bodies clutter the floor in rows
a gloom threaded with sighs
yearnings, griefs and lusts
overhead, the silhouette of guard and gun
prowl against the discolored glass
men's hungers, tears, groans

tall expanses, concrete brick, glass
encircle the harsh cement
dull grey against fresh blood
and a circle of gaping mouths
the faces swallowed away
life bleeding away, the blood pooled

only redeeming this crepuscular acesis
one bright voice, bright eyes, welcoming flesh
one bright ribbon in the encircling gloom
long torn, long lost and tattered
but still cherished at the center of the brain

No, it redeems nothing
cannot stave off the end
nor offer any relief from this
encompassing gloom

FOR WCJB

My brother, who died in exile

For him the battle never ended
he wore doggedly day after day
the armour of isolation and loneliness
the mask of indifference and impassivity
but a slow fury smoldered in his head
and a bitter green fire burnt in his gut like bile

he heard, his anger flaring, each fresh distant outrage
and on the neighbor allies of oppression
his contempt ran in a steady stream like spittle:
even at the end, when his eyes clouded,
the last pinpoint gleam held steady,
and his ragged fragmented lungs rasped, *"Freedom."*

THE FORT PRISON

For NCADP and John Spenkelink, May 26, 1989

They called the single cell
over the doorway
simply *"the condemned."*
Here, prisoners were kept
who could be hanged
(but Gandhi, they said
was also isolated there).
Light was prismed through a fine mesh
so it broke, iridescent,
on the grey wall—
patches of rainbow light delighted me
but I saw how a life could shatter,
be lost into eternity.

ALL VOICES

*Sedako was a young girl who died of the
effects of the atomic bombing of
Hiroshima.*

Sedako's voice is pleading
the voices of millions of children are pleading
"Please let us live."
In the voices of the nightwind
around the corners of the houses
they are calling out
in the murmurs of millions of raindrops
sifting down in the soft spring rain
they are begging
in the winds howling down from the
mountain peaks
or roaring through the trees in the forest
in the stormwinds wailing across the
rooftops;
the voices of children are pleading
"Please let us live."

NAMES

Names in the news
names in the air
Kwazakele, Zwide
Kwanobuhle
strange-sounding to some
familiar to me
names of far-away places
places dear to me:
and dear are the dead who die there
who die struggling to be free:
names in the news
fill the air with sadness
fill the air with tears.

DAYLIGHT

The sunlight comes slowly from the hills
slowly the sunlight drives away the dark
the grey around the townships
is softly touched by the light
slowly the daylight comes

The day will come
The light will come
Peace and joy will come
Will come at last.

VOICES OF CHALLENGE

From the dust
from the mud
from the fields
the voices will rise
the voices of challenge.

Do not be mistaken,
make no mistake,
you will think they are asleep.
You will be wrong —
they will arise —
the voices will rise —
the voices of challenge
will challenge you.

The bones of those who died in the bush ,
the blood spilt in the dust of Soweto,
of Sebokeng, of Sharpeville
of Bishu, of Boipatong, of Kwa Mashu
will challenge you
of Langa, Nyanga and KwazaKele
will challenge you.

When there are compromises
they will challenge you
Where there are betrayals
they will challenge you.

Do not rest easy, do not be deceived
those who have suffered and died
those who have sacrificed for freedom
their voices will challenge you

Endlessly, until we are free.

IN REMEMBRANCE

Jim Gale d. 3/4/86

The calm vibrant voice
    is stilled

the resolute efficient manner
    no longer with us

his urgent will lives on
    in our work against oppression

his presence is around us
    the work for freedom
    drives forward.

GENERAL ASSEMBLY: U.N.

Spirits hover here
beseech with urgent voices:
"Help us to be free."

EXILE

West Lake, China

Nightingales
in branches
on the hillsides
reflected in the smooth
black mirror of West Lake:
a much-travelled traveller said:
"fairest place in all the world,"
my obdurate heart
resisted stubbornly that beauty,
railing soundlessly
against exile.

INDIAN GROUND

Navajo Reservation

A hot dry wind moves
over blown grass and bare ground
sighs a great sadness.

INHERITORS

We are the little
people, who are ruled for now
by giants, briefly.

ONE WORLD WEEPING

To those huddled figures
draped in cloths
young people, perhaps
even small children

moving through the shadows
and into the darkness of corridors

my heart follows you
impotent, in agony

my hands reach out to you
till my fingers are covered with blood

The world is filled
with soundless weeping.

DUSK

Rapt faces, gleaming eyes
assurance of virtue—
and the autumn dusk drags on

Amalgam of complex feelings:
joy and pain and desire
to escape from pain and guilt—
and the autumn dusk drags on

Pall of smoke and dusk
trailing over reeking shanties
coffins for infants and the aged
torture cells walling students—
and the autumn dusk drags on.

HARVEST

Fall's colors signal
the cycle's onward movement.
Life grows to fullness.

DAWN AT EASTER

After pain and death
from the dark tomb comes bright light:
fragrance of lilies.

MEMORY

Statice, purple and
pink, saltair bright, in the white
beach sand, our footprints.

SONG

For the Sandinistas

I hear you singing
though the barbed wire tears
at your throat
and small wildflowers struggle
among the spent bullet casings:
and steady as starlight gleam
or gun-barrels
shines your resolve—
the Somocistas will never return.

HOPE

In the trimmed hedgerows
bared for winter, one twig shows
a green flag of hope.

TOMORROW

King's Beach, Port Elizabeth

The waves will unroll
their bales of foamlace
on the wetsilk sands
over the stumps of the
"Forbidden" signs:
the barbed wire and
barricades
will be gone.

JAMESON ROAD, GELVANDALE

A township ghetto in Port Elizabeth

Suddenly, those asphalt streets
rain-washed and sun-silvered
imaged for me the essence of the world:

there was this harshness, this ugliness
which remained at the bottom a constant
but there were also those instants
of unearned, unexpected beauty
that momentarily redeemed the world.

FEBRUARY, 1990

Yes, Mandela—
some of us admit embarrassedly
we wept to see you step free
so erectly, so elegantly
shrug off the prisoned years
a blanket cobwebbed of pain and grime:

behind: the island's seasand,
harsh, white and treacherous
ahead: jagged rocks and krantzes
bladed crevices of racism and deceit.

In the salt island air
you swung your hammer, grimly stoic
facing the dim path of interminable years.
Now, vision blurred with tears
we see you step out to our salutes
bearing our burden of hopes and fears
and impress your radiance
on the grey morning air.

ABAFAZI

*"Abafazi" in the Xhosa language
is "women." This poem is dedicated
to Dulcie September (killed at her
Paris office by fascist agents),
Ruth First, and all the heroic
fighting women of South Africa.*

Where the shining Tyumie River
winds down through the
Amatola Mountains, blue—
shadowed in their distances
along the banks stand miles
of waving corn, the blade-shaped
leaves flashing as the wind rustles
through them and they throw back like spears
the shafts of light that fall on them:
the trees stand tall, aloof and dreaming in
the haze of the warm midday heat
except for the young blue spruces—
they seem alive and restless with magic
and a blue shade, as if moonlight
lingers there, is gathered around them.

All this grows from dark, rich, fertile soil;
through these valleys and mountain slopes
warriors once poured down to defend
their land and fought and gave their lives:

*they poured their rich blood with fierce
unrelenting anger into this dark fertile soil:
and the men and women fight on,
and give their lives.
The struggle continues.*

TULIPS

Tulips
are immensely sexual:
red tulips
are especially
genital:
their lips pout
half opening, vaginal:
they yearn
with a lustfulness
almost obscene;

They signal beginnings:
now, in hindsight,
I regret that thoughtless
parting gift.

FOR ARTHUR ASHE

Something has gone out
of this world;
there is a sense of loss—
a void—
a great sadness moves
into that empty space
as a vast cloud will
shut out the sun.
He is gone.
That fine man
who made us feel fine—
In time, our sadness
will turn into tears
like a slow, soft,
persistent rain.

SHADES OF RED

For Indira Gandhi, New Delhi

A little breeze
came along
and scattered a few red petals
from the small crumpled red roses
which lay on the raw red brick
that marked her cremation place.

FEBRUARY '64

Leeuwkop Prison, Bryanston, Pretoria

In the cold open dawn
harsh-blue, ice-blue sky
doming overhead
one forgot to be grateful
for late summer's mild
steeling oneself against the icy cold
unaware of a merciful providence.

VIENNA

"Here Schubert Lived"
the guide says
as we pass the painted shutters,
flowering window boxes.
"And here he walked.."
Suddenly the air is filled
with scents of springtime
lilac and melodies;
that swarthy giant's
incandescent shadow still
fills the air with music.

ISLA NEGRA: FOR NERUDA

*Written on the occasion of learning
that Pablo Neruda was to be reburied on
Isla Negra: where he lived.*

Now
the earth that loves you
and that you loved
welcomes you again at last
it's dark brown arms
open to embrace you:

the crowds that swarmed the streets
at your funeral
shouting *"Chile is not dead"*
will shout your return
crying amid tears and laughter
"Presente!"

*"We were waiting for you here
on Isla Negra."*

The sea, the briny kelp, the seagulls
will know that a lover has returned
the scrawled messages to Pablo
on the walls of your shattered house
—all will fill the air with chants and poems

and songs that sing you home.

REMEMBERING

*Wanda Cele, student & poetry
enthusiast, University of Durban–
Westville*

Under these low stars
this sky filled with a red glow,
does this spirit still linger?
is it near in this dusk?
do his eager questions still hover
in this unanswering air?
The gleam of his bright eyes
will find no reflection in this dark:
somewhere, perhaps, red blood turns brown
that oozed from your stab-wound,
your lifeless corpse, all animation gone,
cannot heed our sorrow
nor heal our pain and loss.

PRISON

The "Abyss"* is their word for time,
time in prison—any kind of prison
they can see time as a devouring maw,
a vortex that sucks away their lives;
but in that vision they assert themselves
seeing the abyss and themselves as separate:
so they take on, once more, human dignity.

*Also the name of the Newsletter
published by Pennsylvania Lifers
Association in Huntingdon Prison.
This poem is dedicated to them.*

IDEAS

at Charing Cross, London

We are children of the light
and delight in it,
our bodies revel,
our spirits leap
with sudden scattering of sunlight
through breaking clouds.

We are children of light,
our bodies drink deeply of it—
and as we drink of it we darken
and those who have drunk most deeply are most dark:
their darkness evidence of their love.

We are children, all, of light
our nature is to turn away from the dark,
hate obscurity, fear falsehood.
Joy comes with brightness and clear sight:
it is vision we love, and joy, and truth.

MARTIN LUTHER KING, JR.

A dark silhouette
as dawnlight touches snowfields:
still he waits and dreams.

CATENA

commemorating the victims of Soweto

Pray you, remember them.

The alleys reeking with the acrid stench
of gunfire, teargas and arrogant hate

Pray you, remember them

We remember them

The pungent odor of anger,
of death and dying, and decay

I pray you, do remember them

We remember them

Anger drifting through smoke-filled lanes
in sudden erratic gusts

Pray and remember

We remember them

Torn bodies half-glimpsed
Through standing roiling smoke

Pray, remember them

The ghettos reeking
Fathers grieving
Mothers weeping
Bodies of children torn and bleeding

Pray, remember them:

We remember them

IN MEMORIAM: OLIVER TAMBO

*President of the African National
Congress and its leader during
Nelson Mandela's imprisonment.*

Warrior who has fought the good fight
these long years,
rest easy now.

You who endured
and encouraged others to endure,
rest easy now.

You who could not rest
whose eyes were fixed
on the bright prize of freedom,
rest easy now.

Friend, comrade, counselor
whose quiet guidance directed us,
rest easy now.

You who steered a steadfast path
through the long years of struggle,
now, now at last, rest, rest, rest easy now.